THIS ANNUAL BELONGS TO

~~Margaret~~   ~~Burt Handsome~~

....

BLUEY

LADYBIRD BOOKS

UK | USA | Canada | Ireland | Australia | India | New Zealand | South Africa

Ladybird Books is part of the Penguin Random House group of companies
whose addresses can be found at global.penguinrandomhouse.com.

www.penguin.co.uk   www.puffin.co.uk   www.ladybird.co.uk

 Penguin
Random House
UK

First published 2023
001

 LUDO   **BBC STUDIOS**

Printed in Italy

The authorized representative in the EEA is Penguin Random House Ireland,
Morrison Chambers, 32 Nassau Street, Dublin D02 YH68

A CIP catalogue record for this book is available from the British Library

ISBN: 978-0-241-62235-3

All correspondence to:
Ladybird Books, Penguin Random House Children's
One Embassy Gardens, 8 Viaduct Gardens, London SW11 7BW

 FSC
www.fsc.org

MIX
Paper | Supporting
responsible forestry
FSC® C018179

CONTENTS

MEET THE FAMILY

Say hello to Bluey and her family.

BLUEY

Bluey is a six-year-old kid who loves playing games with her family and friends, and especially with her little sister, Bingo.

SPECIAL TOY

One of Bluey's favourite toys is Polly Puppy.

DAD (also known as Bandit)

Bandit is Bluey and Bingo's dad. He's an archaeologist, which means he gets to dig up a lot of stuff. When he's not at work, he loves to join in Bluey and Bingo's games.

FOOTY FAN

Dad is a big footy fan and loves cricket.

YOU'LL MEET SOME OF BLUEY'S FRIENDS ALONG THE WAY, TOO . . .

6

HONEY

CHLOE

SNICKERS

MUM (also known as Chilli)

Chilli is Bluey and Bingo's mum! She works in airport security, and she knows just how to cheer Bluey and Bingo up when they need it.

SHAKE IT, CHILLI!

Chilli loves music and isn't afraid to shake a move or two!

BINGO

Bingo is Bluey's little sister. She is always up for some fun with Bluey and has a great imagination.

BUG BUDDY

Bingo is an expert bug hunter.

WHO'S IN YOUR FAMILY?

Bingo lives with Mum, Dad and Bluey, but she has lots of other family members, too. Can you name everyone in your family?

PONY-POO PURSUIT!

Uh-oh! Buttermilk has left five pony poos hidden inside this book. Quick – find them before they stink the place out!

COCO

INDY

MACKENZIE

RUSTY

DANCE MODE

Dad is stuck in dance mode! Can you finish each of his dances by using the moves at the bottom of the page? All right, let's boogie!

BATHTIME!

Bluey and Bingo don't want bathtime to be over. Keep the fun going by finding the little pictures in the splashy scene.

1 2 3
4 5 6

LOOKING FOR LETTERS

How many yellow and green letters can you find?

YELLOW   **GREEN**

Now see if you have anything yellow or green in your bathroom!

9

THE DOCTOR

Look how busy Doctor Bingo's waiting room is.
Uh-oh, Rusty's burped up hippos all over the floor!
Check out the picture and use the clues to work
out who Bingo's next patient is going to be.

THIS IS A REAL PICKLE!

THE NEXT PATIENT . . .

is not the doctor.

is not standing on a book.

is not wearing glasses.

is not wearing a jacket.

is not pink.

is not wearing a hat.

TOP TIP

Play Doctors by
asking a friend to be
your receptionist
and book your
appointments!

LOLLIPOP

The doctor still has five patients to see but only one lollipop left.
Follow the lines to find out which patient gets the treat.

NAME: Dr

....

AGE: ....

SPECIAL DOCTOR SKILL:

....

....

You can be a doctor just like Bingo with this ID badge! Remember to draw your picture in the photo space so everyone knows it's you.

Now grab some mates or toys to be your patients. You'll have them fixed in a jiffy!

Ask a grown-up to help you cut out your ID badge and stick it to some cardboard. Don't forget to finish the next page first!

HOW TO DRAW MUFFIN

Muffin is Bluey's cousin. She loves
Moonlight Unicorns and always says what she's thinking.
Follow these steps to learn how to draw Muffin!

1

Start with
her body.

2

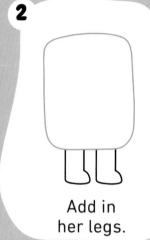

Add in
her legs.

3

Add her
ears.

4

Add her eyes
and nose.

5

Add her tail, arms
and toes.

6

Now add details
to her face.

7

Now add
her spots.

8

Add her eyebrows
and inner ears.

9

Now you can
colour!

TAKEAWAY

Hungry, Squirts? Read about what happened when Dad took Bluey and Bingo to pick up a Chinese takeaway.

1

Dad, Bluey and Bingo are waiting outside the Chinese restaurant for their takeaway order.

GOLDEN·CROWN

TAKEAWAY

OOH, A TAP! CAN I HAVE A SHOWER?

NO WET DOGS IN CAR.

2

Soon, their food is ready. "Can we have some of yours?" Bluey asks Dad. "You don't like spicy food," he replies. "I like spicy!" Bingo says.

BUT WHEN DAD CHECKS THE BAG . . .

"THEY FORGOT THE SPRING ROLLS!"

14

"We're not leaving without the spring rolls. They'll be ready in five minutes," Dad says. "What are we gonna play?" Bluey wonders. "We're gonna play Dad Reads the Newspaper," Dad says.

But . . . Bluey and Bingo get a bit bored waiting for the spring rolls, so they pretend to open their own restaurant. "Welcome!" Bluey smiles, and Bingo takes a mouthful of the takeaway food . . .

"It's tooooo spicy!" she yelps, spitting it out at Dad and dropping it on the floor.

15

6 The takeaway lady comes out with a plate of fortune cookies (they're biscuits with messages hidden inside).

THESE ARE FOR YOU WHILE YOU WAIT.

FLOWERS MAY BLOOM AGAIN, BUT A PERSON NEVER HAS A CHANCE TO BE YOUNG AGAIN.

7 This makes Dad have a little think. "What does it mean?" Bluey asks. "It means . . ." answers Dad.

IT'S SHOWER TIME.

HUH? FOR REAL LIFE?

Dad turns on the tap, and they all have the best time dancing in the water.

SPLASH!

SPLISH!

HA! HEE!

17

THE END

BOB BILBY

It's Bingo's turn to bring Bob Bilby home, and they're having FUN TIMES together. Use your pens and pencils to add lots of colour.

READY, SET, GOANNA!

Bluey and Bingo are racing! Grab a mate, then choose a racer each and see who picks up the most pine cones on the way. Watch out for those bin chickens!

I'LL GIVE YOU A TURBOBOOST!

START

FINISH LINE! FINISH LINE!

CONE COUNTER

Are there any pine cones near where you live? If so, how many can you find?

19

FRUIT BAT

Bluey wishes she was a fruit bat. Fruit bats are 'octurnal nocturnal, which means they sleep during the day and eat fruit all night! Can you find the matching pair?

GO WILD!

What birds, bugs or animals can you see if you go outside at night?

....

....

....

HANGING OUT

In Bluey's dreams, she can hang, eat and even wee upside down, just like a fruit bat! Colour in this picture of her eating some fruit.

CHRISTMAS CRACKERS

Bandit loves telling Christmas cracker jokes! Which ones do you like best?

What did Santa name his pet frog?
Mistletoad!

What do snowmen wear on their heads?
Ice caps!

What do you get if you eat Christmas decorations?
Tinsel-itis!

What do you get if you cross Santa with a duck?
A Christmas quacker!

Why couldn't the skeleton go to the Christmas party?
He had no body to go with!

What do Santa's helpers learn at school?
The elf-abet!

Why are Christmas trees bad at knitting?
Because they lose their needles!

Why did the bush turkey join the rock band?
Because he had drumsticks!

What do you get when you cross a snowman with a vampire?
Frostbite!

What do angry mice send each other at Christmas?
Cross-mouse cards!

Tell these jokes to your family and friends, and see which ones get the biggest laughs.

MAKE YOUR OWN STORIES

It's storytime!
Roll a dice at each square. The number
you roll tells you what happens next!

ONE DAY, A . . .

1 potoroo
2 chickenrat
3 fruit bat
4 granny
5 taxi driver
6 bilby

WANTED TO GO TO . . .

1 the moon
2 the beach
3 the dump
4 play mah-jong
5 Hammerbarn
6 a fancy restaurant

WHEN SUDDENLY . . .

1 they had to go to work
2 they wanted a takeaway
3 they slipped on some beans
4 an emu appeared
5 they went into dance mode!
6 the toilet broke

SO THEY SAID . . .

1 "BEANS!"
2 "How rude!"
3 "Wackadoo!"
4 "They forgot the spring rolls!"
5 "Goodnight!"
6 "It's tickling my bottom!"

AND DECIDED TO . . .

1 dance like no one's watching.
2 go to swim school.
3 build a blanket fort.
4 go camping.
5 have a bush wee.
6 go to bed.

Fill in the gaps below to remember your fave story.

ONE DAY, A _____ WANTED

TO GO TO _____ WHEN

SUDDENLY _____

SO THEY SAID _____ AND

DECIDED TO _____ .

Now you can draw your favourite bit!

27

TAKEAWAY

Oh biscuits! They forgot the spring rolls! Can you spot ten differences between these two pictures while you wait for them to cook?
But be quick – they'll be ready in five minutes!

PUZZLE PIECES

Bingo has some missing puzzle pieces stuck to her bum! Can you work out which three pieces she needs to finish her puzzle off?

1

2

3

4

5

6

JOIN THE STARS

Mum is taking Bluey and Bingo for a night-time bush wee.
Join the stars in the night sky while you wait for them to finish up.
What can you see?

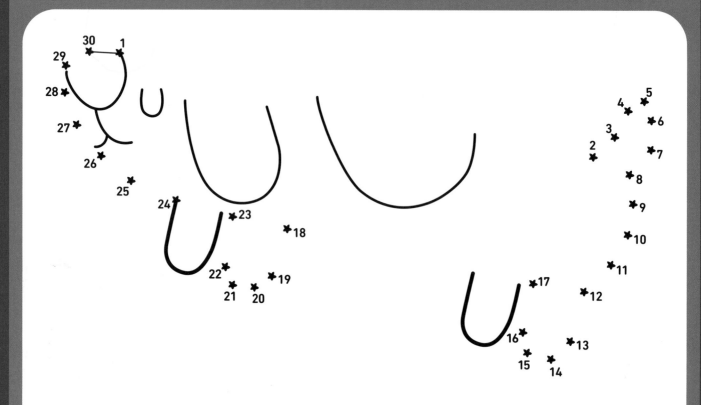

How about adding some planets and stars?

FAIRIES

Beans on toast! The fairies have trapped lots of the Heelers' things inside fairy rings! To break their spell: look carefully at this page for two minutes and try to remember EVERYTHING. When you're ready, turn the page . . .

Careful not to get too close or you might start dancing!

Now look in the fairy rings on this page, and see if you can spot what has changed. Remember, you're not allowed to look back at the previous page – let's do this!

CURSE YOU, FAIRIES!

Wanna make your own fairy ring? Head outside and place rocks, leaves and flowers in a big circle. Now dance around it to seal the spell!

ARMY

Attention! Rusty and his new friend Jack are playing Army.
Help them reach the tree house through the long grass,
but watch out for bush turkeys!

START

FINISH

WE MADE IT!

HAMMERBARN

Bluey and Bingo met their new gnome husbands at Hammerbarn. Find a friend, and design your own gnome husbands here. Don't forget to give them both shovels!

HELLO, HUSBAND.

What kind of funny moustaches will you give your husbands – fancy curly ones or big bushy ones? Will they have shiny buckles? Make sure you give them names!

WHAT A LOVELY VEGGIE PATCH, HECUBA.

KIDS

Who is being naughty at the supermarket?

1

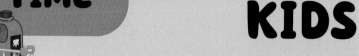

Bluey, Bingo and Dad are off to the supermarket. "Who's your favourite: me or Bingo?" Bluey asks Dad. "You're both my favourites," he replies.

> PARENTS DON'T PICK FAVOURITES.

2 "Hey, Bingo, let's play Kids!" Bluey says. "I'll be Mum, you can be a toddler called Snowdrop and Dad can be the older brother called . . . Diddums!" Mum (Bluey) grabs the shopping list from Diddums (Dad). "I'm in charge of the trolley. Kids can use those little ones." She giggles.

> THAT'S YOUR TROLLEY.

3 Mum starts filling the big trolley with Snowdrop's favourite things (like chocolate milk) while Diddums tries to buy the actual, real-life stuff.
"Can we get some vegetables?" he asks.
"Of course not!" Mum replies.

4 **Soon** . . . Snowdrop starts being a bit naughty, throwing things on the floor.
"Diddums!" Mum gasps, thinking it was him.
"It wasn't me. It was Snowdrop! You always take her side!" Diddums cries.

5 So . . . Mum puts Diddums in a timeout on the toilet-paper chair. "What about Snowdrop?" Diddums asks.
"Snowdrop is my favourite," Mum replies.
"Oh . . . I see . . ." Diddums says sadly.

But Mum begins to feel bad . . . especially when Snowdrop throws greeting cards everywhere.

6 "You were right. It was Snowdrop being naughty all along," Mum says. "I'm sorry I didn't believe you . . . and that I said she was my favourite." She gives Diddums a big hug. "I love you, Mum," he says.

7 But now it's really time to do some shopping! "Diddums, can I put you in charge of the trolley, cos I've got a cheeky toddler to sort out!" Mum says. And soon the shopping is all done. Diddums has been so helpful!

GAHHH!

AHAHAHA!

8 "What a fine young boy you have," the checkout lady says.
"Thank you. He's my favourite." Mum smiles. "Oh, I mean, both my kids are my favourites!" she adds, just in time to see Snowdrop row-row-rowing along the conveyor belt.

WELCOME

SNOWDROP!

THE END

GRANNIES

Oh dearie! Rita's slipped on her beans!
Use your pens and pencils to colour them in.

Bean ~~FOOD~~ SEARCH

Rita and Janet need to pick up lots and lots of beans for dinner. Have a look at the grid below, and circle all the cans of beans you can find. That's lovely, dearie!

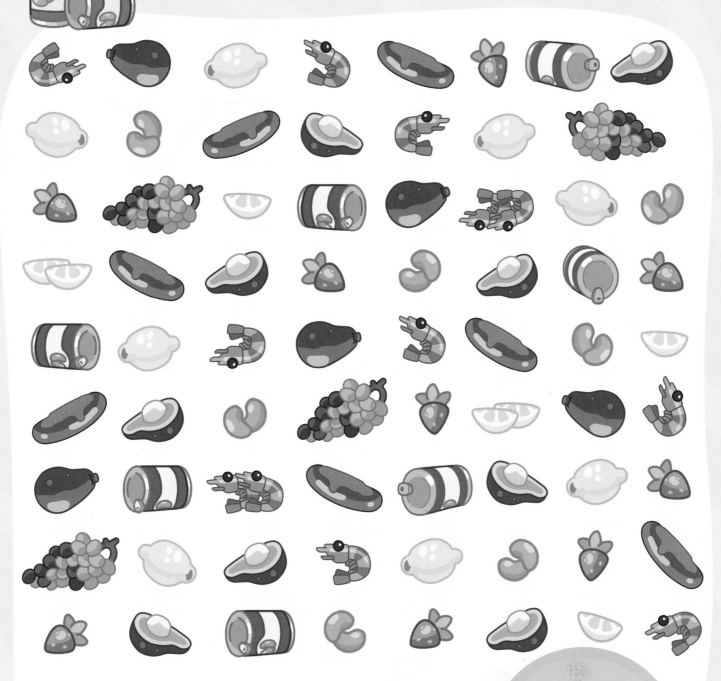

How many cans of beans did you find in the search?

....

Write the answer in the space above, and then shout it nice and loud so the grannies can hear.

There's some sneaky sausages hiding in the grid, too! Yell **"SAUSAGE!"** when you find one!

FANCY RESTAURANT

Hey, chef!
(Yes, that's you!)
What's the special?
Grab some paper and
pens, and make your
own menu. Don't
forget to make
it fancy!

Mum and Dad have gone out to a Fancy Restaurant for a "romance" dinner. The chef has made them something REALLY special. Can you spot ten differences between these two pictures?

YOU WILL BE SERVED BY

MENU 💜
STARTER

_____

MAIN MEAL

_____

DESSERT

_____

MAKE SURE TO ASK
ABOUT THE SPECIAL.

DAD'S ON THE DUNNY!

Oh no, Dad's in a rush to get to the dunny – draw him quick!
What do you think he ate?

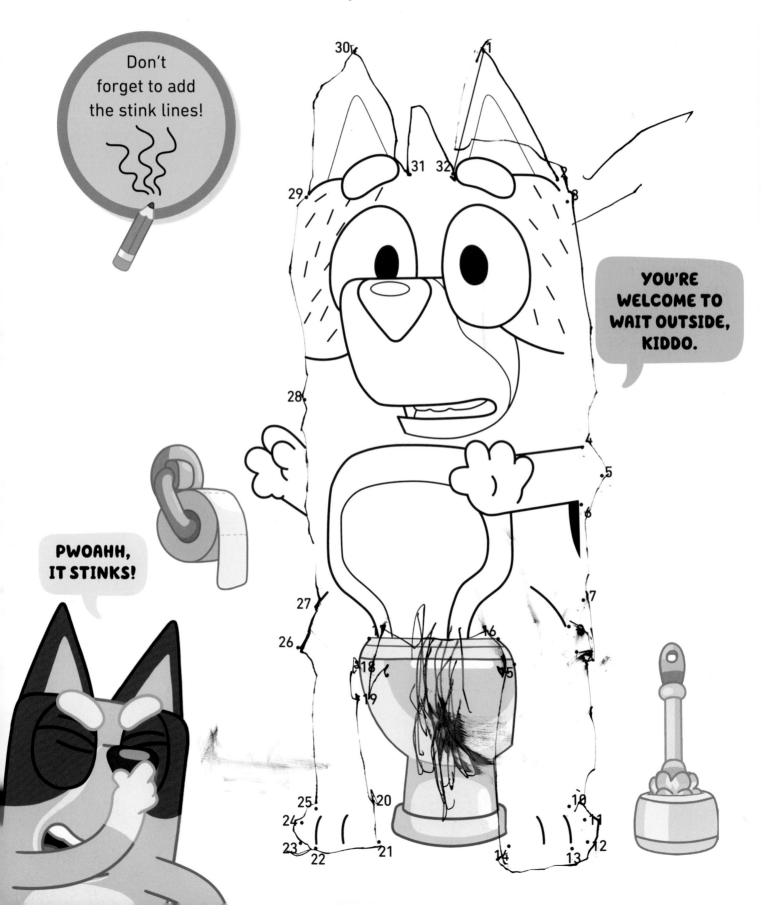

NAIL SALON

It's Stumpfest, but Bluey, Bingo and Muffin have opened up a nail salon. Grab some pencils or crayons, and finish their pretty colour patterns before Dad digs up their salon stump!

45

TAXI

Beep! Beep! Anyone need a taxi? Bluey's customer needs to catch a flight from the airport. Follow the sat-nav instructions to get him there on time.

1 From the starting space, move **RIGHT** two spaces to pick up a rich lady.

2 Continue **UP** on this road for seven spaces.

3 The sat-nav recognizes stumblytastics. Move two spaces **RIGHT**.

4 Wrong turn! Go **DOWN** three spaces.

5 Beans on toast! This is the zoo not the airport! Go **RIGHT** four spaces.

6 Grannies on the road! Wait for them to cross, then go **UP** five spaces.

7 Argh, out of petrol! The customer will have to go the rest of the way on foot! Walk three spaces **RIGHT**.

8 The airport must be around here somewhere! Run two spaces **UP** to catch the flight!

WHERE TO, CUSTOMER?

START

FINISH

47

SEARCH AND FIND

CAN YOU SPOT . . .

tomato sauce

pavlova

What's up, party people? The Heelers are celebrating!
Can you find all the bits and bobs below?

juice

toy car

kookaburra

ball

STORYTIME

BBQ

Err, did someone order a salad?

1

The family is having a BBQ today, and Bluey is playing BBQ with her cousins. Bingo can't wait to relax, but Muffin spots a bowl of salad . . .

SIZZLE . . .

WELL, I WAS RELAXING IN MY RELAXING CHAIR, BUT OK . . .

"We have to have pepper salad with our BBQ!" Muffin says. "Can you be in charge of the salads?" Bluey asks Bingo.

2

Bingo uses Dad's hat as a salad bowl. **"GLEEEN PEPPER!"** Socks cheers. Bingo finds some green leaves they can use for peppers.

After that, she sits in her chair. "Ahhh, so relaxing . . ."

3 "Can I have yellow pepper?" Bluey asks. There are yellow flowers in the hanging basket, but Bingo can't quite reach them. She throws a ball to knock them down. **Yesss!**

Bingo tosses the yellow petals in the hat salad bowl and flops into her chair. "There you go: yellow peppers. Now I'm gonna relax," sighs Bingo.

4 "My favourite colour pepper is red pepper," Muffin says. So Bingo uses a rake to knock down the tree's red flowers.

She dumps the red flowers in the hat bowl and huffs down into her chair. "I don't think there are any more colours of peppers, so I'm going . . . to . . . relax."

51

WHOOOOOSH!

SHE CAN'T TURN THE WATER OFF!

5 BUT...

Muffin notices something is missing. "We need salad dressing!" she tells Bingo. "OK," Bingo groans and turns on the hose to make some yummy (sort of) muddy salad dressing...

SPLOSH!

The hose flies about, spraying water everywhere! Finally, Bingo shuts it off and sits down. "My goodness, this is not relaxing," she says.

IT'S TICKLING MY BOTTOM!

HAHA!

6

"Whose muddy footprints are these?" Mum asks. So Bingo has to mop the floor! She is getting REALLY tired now!

And finally... she can... relax... in her chair...

7 "BBQ's ready!" Dad cheers. The family rushes to the table and digs in to the sausages. *Mmm! Mmm!* Bingo waits. And waits. And waits.

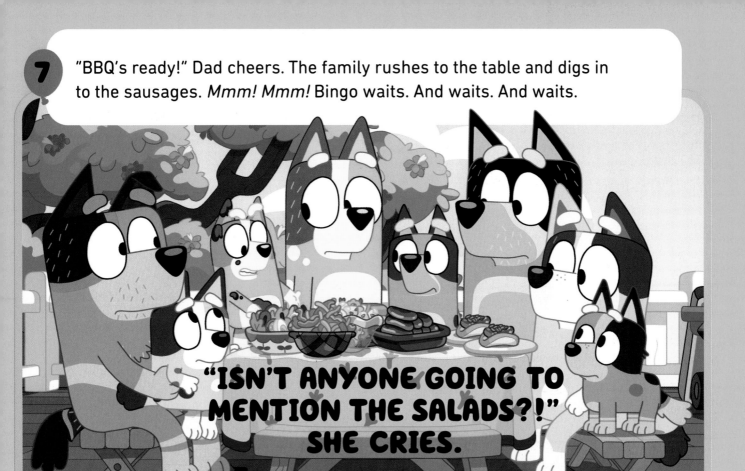

8 "Ah! Amazing! Great!" everyone cheers and claps. Bingo lets out a huge sigh. "Thanks, Bingo," Mum says, giving her a cuddle. **"NOW RELAAAX . . ."**

THE END

THE BIG BLUEY QUIZ

Hooray! You've made it all the way to the end of the book. It's time to find out how well you know Bluey and her family with this Big Bluey Quiz.

1
What is Bluey's dad's job?

A. Firefighter
B. Archaeologist
C. Garden gnome

2
What kind of piñata do the Heelers have at their party?

A. A duck
B. A donkey
C. A bin chicken

3
Where does Bluey's customer need to go in the taxi?

A. The airport
B. Hammerbarn
C. The train station

4
What is the picture on Bingo's jigsaw puzzle?

A. A dinosaur
B. A duck cake recipe
C. A world map

5
What kind of shop do Bluey, Bingo and Muffin open at Stumpfest?

A. A food truck
B. A nail salon
C. A travel agency

6
What does Bluey's dad serve at the BBQ?

A. Sausages
B. Burgers
C. Beans

7

What animal does Bluey
dream of being?

A. A pony
B. A monkey
C. A fruit bat

8

How many lollipops does
Doctor Bingo have left?

A. One
B. Two
C. Three

9

Where does Dad take Mum
for a "romance" dinner?

A. The park
B. A Fancy Restaurant
C. The creek

10

What are Rita and Janet
having for dinner?

A. Mashed potato
B. Biscuits
C. Beans

11

What sport does
Mum play?

A. Hockey
B. Football
C. Keepy Uppy

12

What does the takeaway lady
forget to give Dad?

A. His change
B. Fried rice
C. Spring rolls

HOW DID YOU DO?

Check your answers on page 59. You get one point for every correct
answer. How many did you get right?

1–4 points
Not bad. It was trifficult! You'll do better next time.

5–8 points
Good one! You know heaps about Bluey and her family!

9–12 points
WACKADOO! Well played! You're a star.
Have a can of beans to celebrate.

55

ANSWERS

How did you go?
Check your answers here!

PAGE 7

The stinky pony poos are hidden on pages 9, 19, 23, 49 and 55.

PAGE 8

PAGE 9

PAGES 10–11

PAGE 19

Bingo = 12, Bluey = 14.
Bluey is the winner.

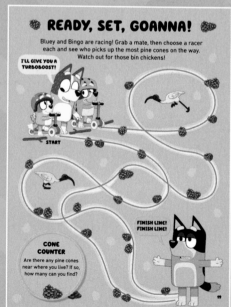

PAGE 20

FRUIT BAT

Bluey wishes she was a fruit bat. Fruit bats are 'octurnal' nocturnal, which means they sleep during the day and eat fruit all night! Can you find the matching pair?

GO WILD!
What birds, bugs or animals can you see if you go outside at night?

....

....

....

PAGE 28

TAKEAWAY

Oh biscuits! They forgot the spring rolls! Can you spot ten differences between these two pictures while you wait for them to cook? But be quick – they'll be ready in five minutes!

PAGE 29

PUZZLE PIECES

Bingo has some missing puzzle pieces stuck to her bum! Can you work out which three pieces she needs to finish her puzzle off?

PAGE 30

JOIN THE STARS

Mum is taking Bluey and Bingo for a night-time bush wee. Join the stars in the night sky while you wait for them to finish up. What can you see?

How about adding some planets and stars?

PAGE 32

Now look in the fairy rings on this page, and see if you can spot what has changed. Remember, you're not allowed to look back at the previous page – let's do this!

CURSE YOU, FAIRIES!

Wanna make your own fairy ring? Head outside and place rocks, leaves and flowers in a big circle. Now dance around it to seal the spell!

PAGE 33

ARMY

Attention! Rusty and his new friend Jack are playing Army. Help them reach the tree house through the long grass, but watch out for bush turkeys!

START

FINISH

WE MADE IT!

MORE ANSWERS

PAGE 41

PAGES 42-43

PAGE 44

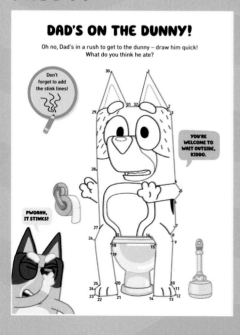

PAGE 45

PAGE 47

SEARCH AND FIND

What's up, party people? The Heelers are celebrating! Can you find all the bits and bobs below?

CAN YOU SPOT . . .

tomato sauce   pavlova   juice   toy car   kookaburra   ball

48
49

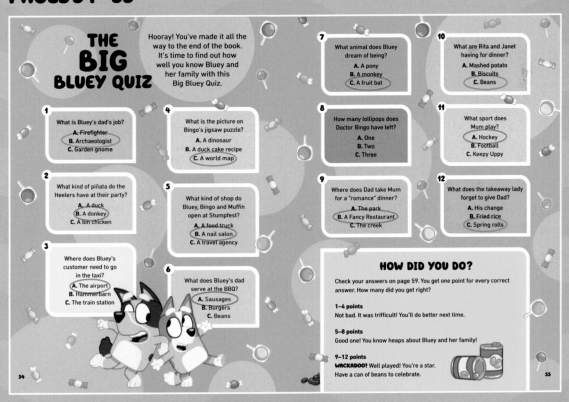

THE BIG BLUEY QUIZ

Hooray! You've made it all the way to the end of the book. It's time to find out how well you know Bluey and her family with this Big Bluey Quiz.

1 What is Bluey's dad's job?
A. Firefighter
B. Archaeologist
C. Garden gnome

2 What kind of piñata do the Heelers have at their party?
A. A duck
B. A donkey
C. A bin chicken

3 Where does Bluey's customer need to go in the taxi?
A. The airport
B. Hammerbarn
C. The train station

4 What is the picture on Bingo's jigsaw puzzle?
A. A dinosaur
B. A duck cake recipe
C. A world map

5 What kind of shop do Bluey, Bingo and Muffin open at Stumpfest?
A. A food truck
B. A nail salon
C. A travel agency

6 What does Bluey's dad serve at the BBQ?
A. Sausages
B. Burgers
C. Beans

7 What animal does Bluey dream of being?
A. A pony
B. A monkey
C. A fruit bat

8 How many lollipops does Doctor Bingo have left?
A. One
B. Two
C. Three

9 Where does Dad take Mum for a "romance" dinner?
A. The park
B. A Fancy Restaurant
C. The creek

10 What are Rita and Janet having for dinner?
A. Mashed potato
B. Biscuits
C. Beans

11 What sport does Mum play?
A. Hockey
B. Football
C. Keepy Uppy

12 What does the takeaway lady forget to give Dad?
A. His change
B. Fried rice
C. Spring rolls

HOW DID YOU DO?

Check your answers on page 59. You get one point for every correct answer. How many did you get right?

1–4 points
Not bad. It was trifficult! You'll do better next time.

5–8 points
Good one! You know heaps about Bluey and her family!

9–12 points
WACKADOO! Well played! You're a star. Have a can of beans to celebrate.

54
55

More great BLUEY books to collect!

PICTURE BOOKS

CAMPING

MUM SCHOOL

GOODNIGHT FRUIT BAT

THE BEACH

BOARD BOOKS

BINGO

THE POOL

GRANNIES

ACTIVITY BOOKS

NOVELTY